TI   K

WATERS, F.

THE EMPEROR AND THE
NIGHTINGALE

CUMBRIA HERITAGE SERVICES
LIBRARIES

COUNTY COUNCIL

This book is due to be returned on or before the last date above. It
may be renewed by personal application, post or telephone, if not in
demand.

C.L.18

For Jo Norman with much love and admiration - FW
To Polly, Lucy and Alice - PB

First published in Great Britain in 1999 Bloomsbury Publishing Plc
38 Soho Square, London, W1V 5DF
This paperback edition first published in 2000

A CIP catalogue record for this book is available from the British Library

ISBN 0 7475 4701 7 (paperback)
ISBN 0 7475 3559 0 (hardback)

Designed by Dawn Apperley
Printed and bound by South China Printing Company

1 3 5 7 9 10 8 6 4 2

BLOOMSBURY CHILDREN'S CLASSICS

THE EMPEROR
and the
NIGHTINGALE

FIONA WATERS AND PAUL BIRKBECK

BLOOMSBURY
CHILDREN'S
BOOKS

Many, many moons ago in ancient China there lived an Emperor who possessed untold riches.

His palace was quite the most magnificent in the world. It was made entirely from the finest porcelain, which did not make it the most comfortable place to live in as you always had to be rather careful where you sat. The palace was surrounded by an enormous garden so big that even the Head Gardener was not quite sure where it ended. The garden was filled with the most exotic and beautifully perfumed flowers, all hung with silver bells that tinkled in the breeze. If you walked and walked through the garden, you would eventually come to a dense forest full of tall swaying trees where brightly coloured birds swooped and swirled all day long. The trees were reflected in deep midnight blue lakes which were full of golden carp and wonderful plumed angelfish. And if you still walked and walked for a night and a day under the lofty trees, you would eventually reach a wide harbour where great sailing ships arrived laden with new treasures and many travellers bearing precious gifts for the Emperor.

Now, high in the branches of the shady trees in the forest, there lived a small nightingale who sang every evening to the poor fishermen as they pulled up their nets. Her song was the most glorious ever heard, full of trills and ripples like flowing water, and whoever heard her had to stop what they were doing and just listen. Many were the travellers and explorers who came to seek out the Emperor and to marvel at his fabulous wealth and delicate porcelain palace and magnificent gardens full of tinkling flowers. When they returned home, however, to write up their learned journals and scholarly tomes, it was the little nightingale they praised the most. Poets wrote long verses seeking to capture the utter magic of her singing, and musicians composed delicate airs dedicated to her. It was not long before word of all this reached the Emperor as he sat stiffly on his great throne. He was not a little put out.

'How is it that this wondrous bird sings in my garden and yet I have never heard her? Why has she been hidden from me?' he demanded crossly. 'Find her at once and bring her to me this evening. I want to hear if she is so very fabulous after all.'

Now truth to tell, although the Emperor loved all his possessions, he was almost too busy to enjoy them – he had never heard the little nightingale because he had never walked through his own garden and did not even know about the forest that swept down to the sea. And all the courtiers had their heads so full of nonsense that they didn't even know what a nightingale looked like, which of course made finding her rather difficult. So they rushed around all day in ever-decreasing circles, but come evening there was no nightingale to present to the Emperor.

'Perhaps she does not really exist but is a figment of the imagination of one of the many visitors to our shores,' suggested one of the bolder courtiers.

The Emperor was very angry.

'I have been sent this book by the Imperial Ruler of Japan, and in it I have read that he has heard a bird who sings like an angel in my garden every night, yet I have never heard it,' said the Emperor. 'I shall chop your heads off if you do not find this nightingale for me.'

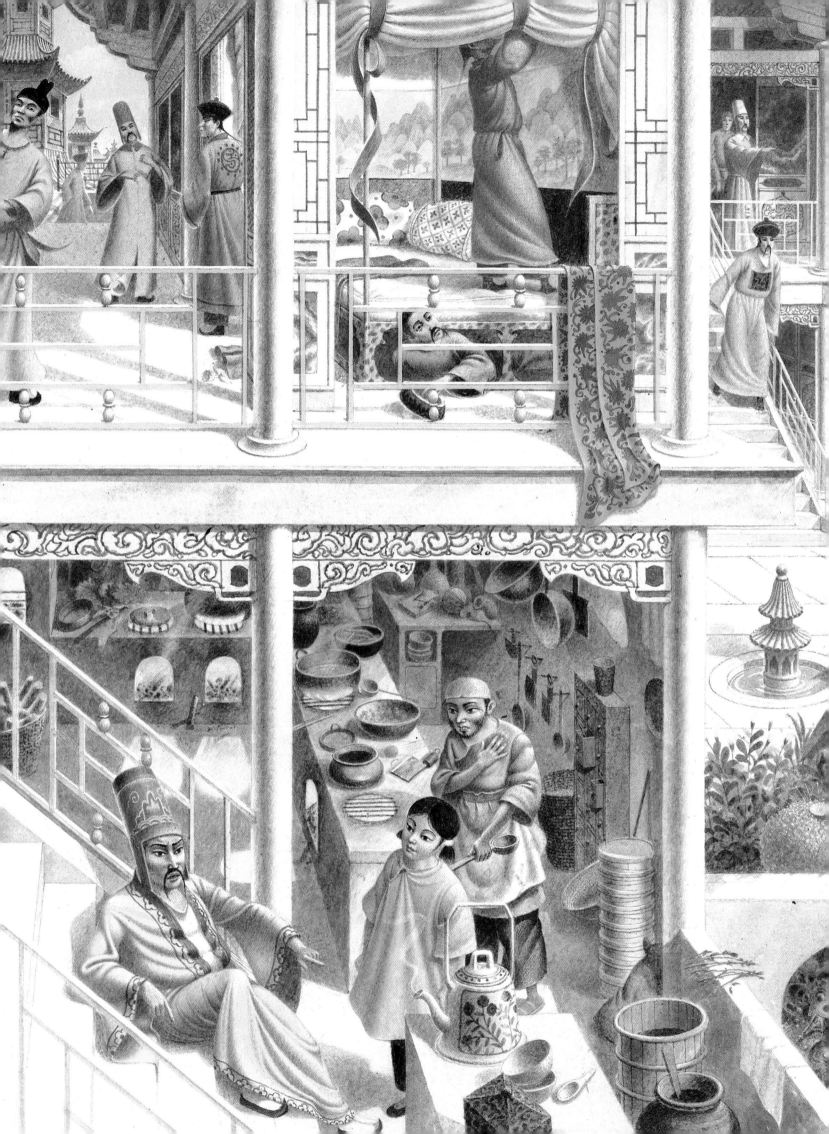

But that was more easily said than done. The next day the courtiers ran up and down the stairs of the porcelain palace, in and out of the offices, through the treasure vaults, round the courtyards, under the vast four-poster beds and between the shelves in the great book-lined library, but of the nightingale they could find no trace. The sun was setting as the Chief Courtier sank into an exhausted huddle in the great palace kitchens, demanding a pot of jasmine tea.

'How can I save my head,' he wailed, 'if I do not even know what this nightingale looks like, let alone find her?'

'Oh, she is easy enough to find,' said a quiet voice from a dark corner of the kitchen.

'Who said that?' demanded the courtier, his tiredness all forgotten.

A small grubby kitchen-maid was pushed forward by the cook.

'I know the nightingale well. She sings for me beautifully whenever I go home to my father the fisherman who lives by the sea.'

'Little kitchen-maid, I shall shower you and your poor father with gold and precious stones if only you will lead me to this bird. She is summoned to attend the Emperor tonight,' cried the distraught courtier.

So a great procession of courtiers and officials and clerks and scribes and musicians and hangers-on, not forgetting the kitchen-maid, all trooped off into the gardens. As they chattered and whooped and shrieked the little kitchen-maid begged them to lower their voices or the little nightingale would be frightened off, but they didn't pay any attention. As the great throng passed a small pond, the frogs began to croak.

'Ah, now I hear the nightingale,' cried the Chief Courtier. 'It is indeed a beautiful sound!'

'Don't be silly,' said the little kitchen-maid. 'That is not the nightingale, it is only the frogs in the pond alarmed by all this noise.'

On and on they went. Suddenly a cow mooed loudly, disturbed by the great procession.

'Marvellous,' murmured the Imperial Poet. 'This nightingale has the most powerful voice, I had not thought it to be so impressive.'

'Don't be ridiculous,' said the little kitchen-maid. 'That is the cow who gives the Emperor his fresh milk.'

By now the great trail of people had reached the forest and quite a few of them were looking decidedly nervous at the thought of walking in under the trees, which looked very forbidding in the dusk.

'Don't be frightened. This is the way I always come and I am never afraid,' said the little kitchen-maid. 'And if you would all be quiet we might even hear the nightingale,' she added rather fiercely.

Even as she ceased speaking the nightingale began to sing.

'Now *that* is a nightingale!' said the little kitchen-maid, pointing up to a small unremarkable brown bird sitting amid the branches of a great old tree.

'But she is so ordinary!' exclaimed the Chief Courtier. 'Perhaps she has lost her colour in her embarrassment at seeing so many people.' (He really was a most pompous man).

'Dear nightingale, our beloved Emperor wants to hear you sing tonight. Will you come back to the palace with me?' asked the little kitchen-maid, quite ignoring the Chief Courtier.

'I should be greatly honoured,' said the nightingale quietly, 'although my song sounds best here in the woods.' But when it was explained to her that the Emperor had insisted, she agreed to return to the palace perched on the little kitchen-maid's shoulder.

As they approached the palace, it looked like a shimmering cloud floating above the garden. All the rooms were filled with candles and the light flickered off the polished porcelain. The silver bells on the flowers tinkled in the breeze and delicate perfumes wafted on the night air. As the courtiers entered the palace, they saw a tiny golden perch beside the Emperor's throne for the nightingale. All the other courtiers were there in their finest silk and brocade robes.

The Emperor himself was seated silently on the throne and he looked very curiously at the drab little bird as she sat amid such magnificence. He nodded towards the nightingale and she began to sing. The glorious liquid sound filled the great hall of the palace and spilled out into the gardens where all the citizens had gathered quietly to listen to this fabled bird. Her voice soared and trilled and the Emperor's eyes filled with tears. He had never heard anything quite so beautiful in all his life. The tears ran down his cheeks and still the plain little bird sang so sweetly it made the heart ache.

When the room finally fell silent, the Emperor bowed deeply to the little nightingale and said, 'From henceforth you shall wear my golden slipper around your neck.' Now this was the highest honour that the Emperor could bestow, but the bird said quietly, 'I have had reward enough. I have seen the tears of my beloved Emperor. I need no other gift.'

But the Emperor ordered that the nightingale be given her own golden cage to live in and a golden silk cushion to sit on, and to be taken outside with a golden chain around her leg by one of the court ladies. And every night she was led into the great hall to sing to the Emperor, but she pined for the wind on her feathers, and the rough branches of the trees under her feet. She longed for the simple life she had enjoyed before. Deep inside her heart was aching.

One day a very large parcel arrived for the Emperor from far across the seas. Inside an ornate box there lay another nightingale – a mechanical one. It was fashioned out of gold and silver and encrusted with rubies and diamonds and sapphires and had two emeralds for eyes. When it was wound up it sang a fluting song while its tail bobbed up and down.

'Such perfection!' exclaimed the Emperor. 'Bring me the real nightingale, they must sing together.'

The real nightingale sang as freely as ever while the mechanical bird whirred through its repertoire faultlessly. The Imperial Song Writer pronounced the mechanical bird the better singer because it kept perfect time and of course everyone agreed that it was very much more handsome to look at than the drab little nightingale. The Imperial Music Master declared that at least the mechanical bird would always be available to listen to, unlike the real nightingale. The mechanical bird was set upon the golden perch and surrounded with costly gifts and cushions, and everyone declared the sound the most melodious they had ever heard.

And what of the poor little nightingale? In all the commotion no one noticed her fly out of an open window, up, up into the sky and away back to the forest. Oh, how happy she was! And there she sang once more to the fishermen at night as they lifted their nets, and she sang to the little kitchen-maid who had also been forgotten in all the to-ing and fro-ing at the court.

Ayear and a day went by. In the evening the Emperor was listening to the mechanical bird as usual when suddenly, with a harsh grating sound and a clang, the jewel-encrusted bird broke into two halves! The Emperor leapt to his feet in dismay and summoned the Imperial Watchmaker. After much tinkering and tapping and head shaking, he declared sadly that the bird was broken beyond repair. It was a major tragedy. The Emperor was utterly desolate, what would he do without his singing bird? No one remembered the real nightingale except the little kitchen-maid and she decided to keep quiet this time.

Years passed and the Emperor fell gravely ill. He was by now an old man and although everyone loved him, it was felt that he would not live

for very much longer so a new Emperor was chosen. Everyone at court had rushed off to pay their respects. A deep silence reigned. The old Emperor lay lonely and deathly pale and cold. The marble floors were covered with great black rugs so that no noise should disturb him and the heavy velvet curtains were pulled close. A window was open and the wind stirred the golden tassels round the bedposts, and a shaft of moonlight fell onto the golden bed.

But the Emperor was not dead yet. His breath was laboured and his head ached. His mind was filled with fear as he remembered his life which had seen its fair share of good and bad deeds.

'Music, music. Please play me music to ease my mind and to take away my fears,' he cried, but there was no one around to hear him. All he could hear was his own rasping breathing. 'Please will someone sing to me one last time?' he pleaded and suddenly the most heavenly sound filled the darkened room. A sweet and glorious song – it was the little nightingale, sitting outside the window on the bough of an overhanging tree. She had heard that the Emperor was reaching the end of his life and decided that she would sing to him one last time. As she sang it seemed to the Emperor that the blood coursed through his veins more strongly and his eyes grew less dim. The room was filled with the heady perfumes from his garden and even the darkest shadows retreated in the full beam of moonlight. On and on the little bird sang until the Emperor sank into a deep and refreshing sleep.

She stayed by his side all through the long night and she was there when he awoke fully restored in the morning. The sun was flooding into his room and he flung back the heavy curtains and breathed deeply on the pure fresh air.

'Dearest little bird, how can I ever repay you?' he asked. 'I do not deserve your devotion after I cast you aside for a mere mechanical toy.'

'I do not need any payment,' said the nightingale. 'As I have said before, I have seen the Emperor's tears and I shall never forget that. I have no need for jewels and silken cushions, I only wish to sing to my beloved Emperor.'

'Stay with me always,' pleaded the Emperor. 'I could not bear to lose you again, and I owe you my life.'

But the bird shook her head.

'Let me come and visit you as I wish. In the evenings I shall tell you of all that I have seen, of suffering and of great fortune, of good deeds and of bad, and as a wise man you shall act on this information as you see fit. But never tell anyone you have a little bird who tells you everything.' And so saying she flew away out of the window.

When the servants came into the great bedchamber a little while later to pay their last respects to their great Emperor, they were astonished to find him standing by the open window, smiling at them as he said, 'Good morning!'